WRITTEN BY
MARY GROSSNICKLE

ILLUSTRATIONS BY
ALISON RELYEA

PUBLISHED BY
SPEAKING OF ADOPTION

Adoption is love forever!
Mary Grossnickle

ISBN 0-9762396-0-4

Published by
Speaking of Adoption
www.speakingofadoption.com

Printed in the United States of America
First printing: October 2004

10   9   8   7   6   5   4   3   2   1

Dedication

To all my parents

As soon as the sun came up each morning,
Charlie bolted out the door of his house
and headed for the woods.

He couldn't wait to get out and run!

"Whee!"
Charlie cried as he sailed over a dead log.

He darted under piles of brush and
sprinted between rocks and through mounds of leaves.

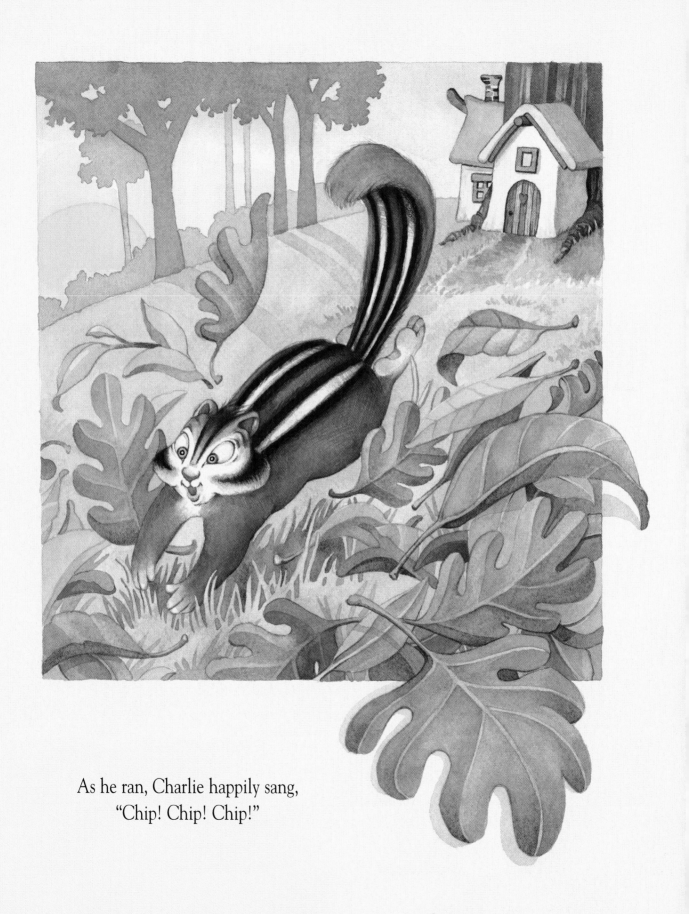

As he ran, Charlie happily sang,
"Chip! Chip! Chip!"

After his morning run, Charlie found an oak tree
with plenty of plump acorns.
When he packed the acorns into his mouth,
his cheeks were as big as his whole head!

With his cheeks full of acorns,
he raced home to share the food with
his mother and father and his brother and two sisters.

"Chip! Chip! Chip!" Charlie cheerfully called.
They all came running and gathered around the pile of acorns.

"This is yummy," Charlie's brother said as he gobbled his breakfast.
"For a little guy, you sure bring home a lot of food!"

"A little guy,"
Charlie thought crossly as he munched a big acorn.
"I'm always the littlest."

It was true.
Charlie was the smallest
member of the family.

He was short and brown, and he had
black and white stripes down his back.
His tail was thin and furry.

Max —
Libby —
Abby —

Char

His mother and father
and brother and sisters were
taller and chubbier than Charlie.

Everyone except Charlie was gray,
with no stripes at all,
and their tails were big and bushy.

That night when Charlie's mother
was tucking him into bed, Charlie asked,
"Mommy, why don't I look like you and Daddy?"
Charlie already knew the answer,
but he liked to hear his mother tell the story.

Charlie's mother said,
"Well, you grew inside a different mother's tummy.
She is called your birthmother. And you have a birthfather, too.
You probably look like they do."

"Why don't I live with them?" Charlie asked.

"Your birthmother and birthfather weren't ready
to be a mommy and daddy when you were little,"
Charlie's mother replied.
"And we wanted another child.
You came to live with us, and that made us very happy!"

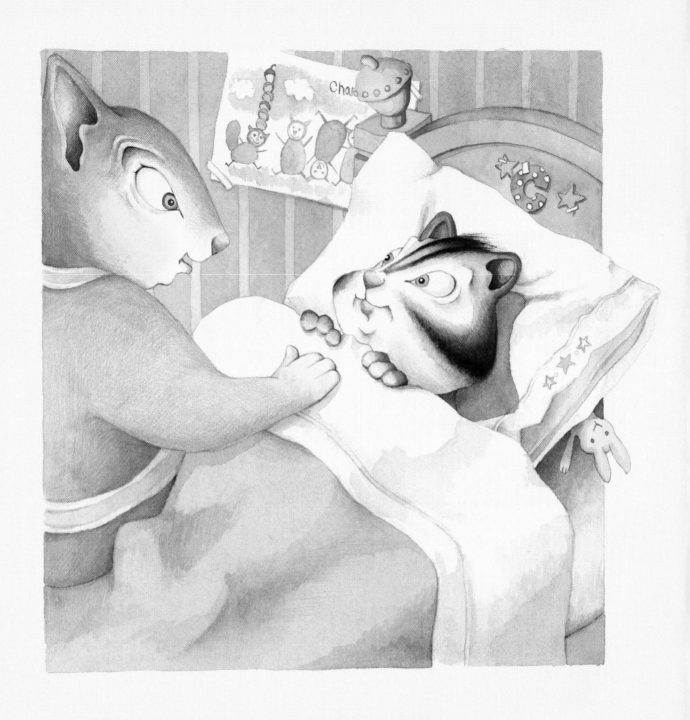

Charlie smiled.
He loved to hear about how he joined his family.

Suddenly he wrinkled his brow
and asked,
"Does that mean I have two mothers and two fathers?"

"Well," his mother answered,
"you have a birthmother and birthfather who made you.
And you have a forever Mother and forever Father."

"I know who that is!" Charlie exclaimed.
"That's you and Daddy!
You are my forever Mommy and forever Daddy."

"That's right, Charlie.
We are your forever family."
His mother smiled as she gave him a big hug.

Charlie hugged his mother and said,
"I'm glad you're my forever family,"
and then he yawned and rubbed his eyes.
"Good night, Mommy."

"Good night, Charlie.
I love you,"
his mother said as she closed his door.

"I love you too, Mommy," Charlie said quietly.
But Charlie couldn't fall asleep.

He folded his arms behind his head and thought for a long time.

The next day Charlie didn't feel like running.

He didn't sing,
"Chip! Chip! Chip!"

And he didn't gather acorns for breakfast.

Instead, he walked slowly
to his thinking place,
an old hollow log at the edge of the woods.

He laid his head on his little brown paws and peered out.
Charlie had a lot to think about.

He had a birthmother and a birthfather.
And he had a forever Mommy and a forever Daddy.

"I know what Mommy and Daddy look like," Charlie thought.

"But I wonder what my birthmother and birthfather look like.
Do I look like them?"

Charlie stayed in his thinking place
almost all morning
and thought
about his birthmother and birthfather.

"I wonder what their names are,"
Charlie murmured.

Turning over on his back, Charlie watched the clouds.

"I bet my birthmother is beautiful,"
he sighed.

"Maybe my birthfather
is famous.
He could be a sports star!"

When his brother and sisters
begged him to come and play,
Charlie finally scampered out to join them.

But instead of playing,
he bit his brother on the nose.
He teased his sisters and pulled their tails.

No one was having much fun,
and they were glad when they heard their mother call,
"Lunchtime!"

During lunch,
Charlie played with his food.
He forgot to say please and thank you.

He didn't use his napkin,
and he spilled his milk.

And his mother had to ask him
three times
to keep his elbows off the table.

Charlie's mother knew
that something was troubling him.
After lunch, she sat down in her favorite chair
and pulled him onto her lap.

"Charlie, honey," she said,
"I think you're having a tough day today.
Sometimes you look mad, and sometimes you look sad."

Charlie curled into a little ball on his mother's lap.
He didn't know what to say.

"Last night we talked about
your birthmother and birthfather,"
she softly continued,
"and I wonder
if you've been thinking about them."

Charlie looked up at his mother.
"Well, maybe,"
Charlie said in a voice so quiet it was almost a whisper.

"It's OK to think about your birthmother and birthfather,"
Charlie's mother said.

Charlie snuggled in his mother's arms.
Then he said in a quiet little voice,
"I wonder
if they think about me."

"I'm sure they think about you, Charlie,"
his mother replied as she kissed the top of his head.
"You have a very special place in their hearts."

"Maybe
they don't have room in their hearts for me,"
Charlie said sadly.

"We have room in our hearts
for everybody we care about, Charlie,"
his mother said wisely.

"I'll show you what I mean."

Charlie's mother found two very large pieces of red paper.
She cut each piece into a giant heart.

"This is your heart," she explained, handing Charlie one of the hearts.
"And this is my heart."

"I'm going to write the names of everyone I keep in my heart,"
Charlie's mother said as she started to write.

Soon her heart was so full that she had
to write some names on top of other names!
Charlie tried to count the names,
but there were too many.

"Now it's your turn, Charlie.
Who has a place in your heart?" she asked.

Charlie said, "You and Daddy."
He wrote Mommy and Daddy in very big letters in the middle of the heart.

"And my brother and sisters," Charlie said.
He concentrated and wrote Abby and Libby and Max.

Charlie wrote Grandma and Grandpa, then Aunt Sophie and Uncle Chester.
He wrote the names of all his cousins and all his friends.

Finally he set down his pencil.
"Whew!
I think I'm done," he said.

"Look at all the people we care about, Charlie," his mother said.
"And they care about us, too.
Isn't it wonderful?"

Charlie's mother looked at him tenderly and asked,
"Is there anyone else you'd like to add?
Maybe someone you've been thinking about lately?"

Charlie sat and stared at his red paper heart.

"Well," Charlie finally said,
"I have my birthmother and my birthfather."

"But I don't think about them all the time. I just *wonder* about them sometimes.
Besides, my heart is pretty full already."

"The best thing about hearts, Charlie," his mother said,
"is that they can never be too full."

"I'm not sure, Mommy," Charlie said.
"I don't want to make
you and Daddy sad by giving my
birthmother and birthfather a
place in my heart."

"Oh, Sweetie," said Charlie's mother.
"That wouldn't make us sad."

Charlie hesitated.
"Are you sure, Mommy?"

"Yes," his mother answered gently, "I'm very sure."

"OK, Mommy," he said as he wrote.
"Then I'd like to give my
birthmother and birthfather a place in my heart."

After he finished writing, he looked up at his mother.

When he saw her smiling,
Charlie's face broke into a huge grin.

Through the open window came the sounds of a wild game of tag.

Charlie heard someone yell,
"Charlie, come and play!"

Charlie jumped up.
His eyes sparkled, and he gave his mother a quick hug.

"I'm going outside now, Mommy,"
Charlie called
as he dashed toward the door.
"I love you a whole bunch, Mommy. Bye!"

And he scampered off singing,
"Chip! Chip! Chip!"

Mary Grossnickle was adopted as a toddler.
She provides post-adoption information and
support to adoptive families in Wisconsin,
where she lives on a lake and is visited frequently
by chipmunks and squirrels.

Visit her at **www.speakingofadoption.com**

Alison Relyea lives in a small town
near Madison, Wisconsin, with
her husband, child, and two tabby cats.

Visit her at **www.alisonrelyea.com**